PARTY HATS FOR SWEET MINOTAURS

AN OBSCURE ACADEMY STORY

LAURA GREENWOOD

True feelings come to light when a minotaur plans a birthday party.

When Sage's birthday plans fall through, she's disappointed, but at least the handsome minotaur who lives in her flat is willing to lend her a supportive ear. If only she could stop thinking about if they could be more.

Castor's feelings for Sage have been growing with every passing moment, so when he has the chance to throw the witch a birthday party, he throws himself into it.

Can the two of them come together over cake and party hats?

-

Party Hats For Sweet Minotaurs is a light-hearted witch academy m/f romance set at Obscure Academy. It features a witch with disappointing birthday plans and a minotaur venturing into party planning.

If you enjoy upbeat and light-hearted paranormal romances with new adult characters, an academy/university setting, guaranteed happy endings, and quirky supernaturals, start the Obscure Academy today!

To FAKA,

Having a writing group is dangerous for my to-do list, and here you all go adding book ideas too!

ONE

SAGE

SOMETIMES IT'S ANNOYING that I have to go all the way down to the kitchen just to make a cup of tea and grab a biscuit. Perhaps I should have taken the half-eaten packet of digestives back to my room yesterday, but I was trying to be reasonable and not scoff a whole packet in one go.

The kitchen door creaks loudly as I push it open. and I wince. I wish building services would hurry up and fix it, I've lost track of the number of requests we've sent to them about it. The same with the broken hob.

"Hey, Sage," Castor says as I walk inside,

turning to face me from his spot hunched over the sink.

"Hi." Heat rises to my cheeks as I take in his handsome face and the two twisted horns that rise up on either side of his head. I know he's self-conscious about them, but I think they make him look cute. "I was going to make some tea, would you like some?"

"I actually boiled the kettle already, there should be enough." He nods towards it as if we don't both live in the flat and are perfectly aware of where things are.

"Oh, thanks." I try not to be too disappointed that it means our time together will be cut short. I make my way over and set my mug down next to his already brewing tea. I flick the kettle back on, mostly out of habit rather than an actual need to.

Castor grabs one of his pots and dunks it into the water with a soft splash.

"I can do that, if you want," I say, nodding to the washing up.

"Oh, it's no problem, I wouldn't want to cause you any work," he responds.

"It wouldn't be any," I assure him, patting the pocket with my wand in it to make it clear that my offer involves magic and not me doing the washing up by hand.

Indecision flits over his face.

"I'll be done in thirty seconds," I promise, though as I say it, I start questioning whether it's a good idea when it means we'll get less time together. But I can't deal with the sight of any of my flatmates washing up when I can do it so easily with just a flick of my wand.

"Okay." He steps back and shakes off his hands, scattering suds all over the floor.

I smile at him, glad he's taken me up on the offer, especially as it means that he trusts me. I withdraw my wand from my pocket and flick it over the sink. Within seconds, his dishes are sparkling clean and stacked on the drying rack. Not that they need to be there, part of my spell ensures that they're ready to go straight back in the cupboard. The satisfaction that always comes from successful magic passes through me.

"That's a handy trick," he says.

"It certainly saves some time," I agree.

The kettle finishes boiling just as Castor goes to put his plates away.

I go to put water in my mug only to realise that I haven't put a tea bag in yet. I reach up to grab a tea bag from my cupboard, turning slightly in the process and ending up face-to-face with Castor without meaning to.

My breathing catches and I bite my lip. For a split moment, I think his gaze drops there, but it's gone so quickly that I'm not so sure it was a real thing or if I'm imagining it because I want it to be true.

Castor clears his throat and pulls away. "Sorry."

I'm too dazed to answer straight away. "My fault," I murmur.

"Are you going to finish your tea?" he asks.

"Oh, right." Despite the tea bag still in my hand, I somehow managed to forget. I drop it into my mug and follow it up with the water.

"Do you mind if I get mine?" Castor says, gesturing past me.

"Oh, yeah." Eurgh, I need to pull myself together. I'm not always so tongue-tied around guys, but Castor just seems to have this effect on me. Maybe it's because of the time I accidentally walked in on him when he'd just gotten out of the shower. I only wanted to ask if he wanted a cup of tea, but I caught him at a bad time. Or a good time, considering I haven't been able to stop thinking about it since.

"Sage?" he asks.

I push the memories aside and step back. "Sorry."

"It's okay." He smiles at me and finishes making his tea.

"How is your assignment going?" I ask, trying to rid myself of the lingering awkwardness of thinking about someone in an inappropriate way when they're in the room.

"The marketing one?"

I nod. "You said you were having a hard time with it."

"Oh, yeah, we're handing it in tomorrow. I'm going to be glad when it's over. Just normal group project stuff. You know what it's like."

I nod. Though I don't seem to have had as much of a problem with it as he's had with his group. I suppose that's the risk when it comes to the randomly assigned groups. I can't say I'm a fan of the system.

The loud creak of the kitchen door breaks through my thoughts, and I curse whoever it is who has decided to enter the room right when I'm actually managing to have a conversation with Castor without making a total fool out of myself.

"Hey, guys," Rhea says with a bright smile as she makes her way inside. One of her snakes slithers out of her bun and onto her shoulder, giving a soft hiss which I assume is his own form of hello.

I smile despite my brief annoyance. Her snakes

are adorable, though I don't imagine she thinks that when she's trying to tame the two of them.

"Hey," I respond to the gorgon.

"I should go," Castor mumbles. "Thanks for doing my dishes, Sage." He looks as if he might say something else, but he simply picks up his tea and leaves the room.

"Why do I feel as if I just walked in on something?" Rhea says, eyeing me suspiciously.

"You didn't," I mutter.

"Ah, but you wish I had." There's no mistaking the knowing expression on my best friend's face.

"Is there any point denying it?"

"Nope. For one, your monster-sized crush is obvious for anyone with eyes," she sings-songs.

"It's not monster-sized."

"All right, your minotaur-sized crush, then."

"Hmm, I suppose it is six-foot-four without the horns," I muse.

"And for two, you told me about it last week when you'd had a couple of vodka cranberries." She opens the fridge and rummages around.

Her snake perks up, clearly wanting a snack.

She sighs dramatically and tears a piece of ham out of the packet and feeds it to the snake.

"Where does that even go?" I ask, my curiosity getting the better of me.

Rhea shrugs and readjusts her glasses.

I look away, knowing she prefers it if we do that when she's fiddling with the glasses that stop her from turning us all into stone.

"I've always assumed it enters my normal digestive system," she says.

"Can you taste it?"

"No."

"Gorgon snakes are weird."

She lets out a bemused snort. "Yeah, the snakes are the weirdest thing about me."

"I think they're pretty cool though."

"I'm not surprised, you have a thing for weird," she teases.

"Hey, Castor's horns aren't weird."

She gives me a knowing smile.

"They're not why I like him," I murmur.

"Mmhmm."

I roll my eyes and turn my attention back to making my tea. This is why I shouldn't have told my best friend anything about the way I'm feeling about our flatmate.

"For what it's worth, he's definitely into you too," she says as she gets a bag of frozen potato smileys out of the freezer.

I scoff. "He does not."

"Has he told you that?" she asks.

"Well, no. I haven't brought it up with him for obvious reasons."

"Then how do you know how he's feeling?" I ask.

"Because he's giving you the same looks that you give him," she responds. "It may not be obvious to you, but it is to everyone else."

"Hmm."

"But if you want to find out for sure, then just ask him." She shrugs as if it's the easiest thing in the world to do so.

I narrow my eyes at her, trying to work out if she's just trying to get me to talk to Castor because she thinks it'll be good for me, or if it's because she actually thinks he's into me.

Do I want to risk asking him and finding out?

"I'll think about it," I mumble. I guess it won't hurt to have a conversation, and it might even turn out better than I think it will.

I just have to figure out how to broach the subject.

TWO

SAGE

My phone lights up and I'm surprised to find Mum's name on the screen. Why is she calling me when I'm going to be seeing her in a couple of days? That's very unlike her.

I hit the answer button, hoping that it isn't going to be anything bad.

"Hello?"

"Sage, hi sweetheart," she greets me in a falsely cheery voice.

"Hi, Mum. What's up?" Worry worms through me at the way she's sounding.

"Oh, I was just calling you to say that Pete and I are going away tomorrow."

"Tomorrow?" My heart drops.

"Yes. I know it's short notice, but he asked if I wanted to go to Paris, and how could I say no?"

How indeed?

I slump down onto the nearest bench and hope that no one notices me having a difficult conversation with her. I suppose that's one advantage of being outside, everyone is wrapped up in their own worlds and don't notice witches having breakdowns on benches. "What about your visit here?"

"Oh, sweetheart, I didn't think you'd mind. You know how long it's been since I've had a holiday. And we can do whatever it is you wanted to another time."

"Mmhmm." My eyes sting with unshed tears. "Okay, well, I hope you have a good time."

"I'm sure I will, sweetie. Bye-bye!" The line goes dead without so much as her asking me how I am.

I sigh and stare at my screen, unsure what to do with myself now. I have lectures to attend, but I can't bring myself to get up and go.

"Is this seat taken?" a familiar voice asks.

I look up to find a pair of concerned brown eyes looking down at me.

"Or I can go if you want," Castor says, gesturing towards the accommodation block we live in.

"Stay." The word comes out barely above a whisper.

He nods and takes a seat next to me. "Want to talk about it?"

"How do you know there's something to talk about?"

"Because I've been living with you for the past, what, seven months?" he checks.

"Something like that," I respond.

"So, want to?"

I let out a loud sigh, realising that as much as I want to talk to him about the way I've been feeling about him, I need my friend more in this situation. "I'm sad about my birthday."

Alarm crosses his face. "We've all forgotten about it, haven't we? If it's today, then I'm sorry."

I chuckle. "It's Friday."

"Okay, so I only slightly forgot about it." Relief flashes over his face.

I snort. "It's not about anyone here," I promise, taking a deep breath. "It's my mum. She promised that because this year was the first one I was away from home, she'd come visit for my birthday and we'd have lunch. We talked about it over the holidays and everything, but she just called and told me that her new boyfriend asked her to go to Paris tomorrow and she said yes."

"Ouch."

"Yeah. And if that's not bad enough, I told Dad I couldn't meet him because I have plans with Mum. Had."

"You could tell him things have changed?"

I sigh. "I could. But I don't want him thinking I only want to see him because Mum bailed on me. It's a no-win situation." I wish I'd never said no to him in the first place, I was just excited about the prospect of spending some time with Mum. We haven't had much of a chance to since she started dating her new guy. Which is sadly normal.

"I'm sorry," Castor says.

I shrug. "Don't be, it's not your fault."

"What are you going to do instead?" he asks.

"No idea. Maybe nothing. I can get some ice cream and a pizza or something. Or Rhea's probably going on a night out, maybe I'll do that. A dance at Jungle might be nice."

"You're not a shifter," he says.

"You don't have to be a shifter to go to Jungle," I point out. "That's just to use the shifting room. They play the best music there."

"Ah."

"You don't think so?"

"I'm not really a *night out* kind of person."

"That's fair," I respond. "Some people just aren't."

"Can I tell you something?" he asks.

"I did just unload how I was feeling on you, I'm all ears." And only partly because I'm curious about what he's going to say.

He glances away. "I'm not sure I should say."

Disappointment fills me, but I reach out and touch his hand. "That's okay. But I'm here to listen if you ever want me to."

His gaze fixates on where my hand is touching his.

"Sorry, I should have asked." I pull my hand away.

Before I can, he takes hold of it. "It's nice."

"Oh." My heart races at the touch, particularly the way his thumb is brushing over the back of my hand. It's certainly making it difficult for me to think straight.

"It's just that one of the reasons I don't like going out is because of all the drunk people."

I frown. "You don't drink? I've never noticed." I think back to the times we've had flat drinks to work out if I've ever seen him with one, but I don't think I've been paying much attention to what everyone else has been choosing to drink. That's not really any of my business.

"I do. It's more the people," he admits.

"Ah, yeah, I can see how drunk people are annoying."

"Particularly with what they say." He lets out a deep sigh. "I always get people coming up to me when they've been drinking and asking if they can touch my horns." He reaches up to one as he mentions it.

"Are you sure they're not suggesting something else?" I ask without thinking.

Castor gives a low chuckle. "Reasonably certain. It's normally followed by a load of questions about what it's like to have them."

"I imagine you think about them as much as you think about your arms."

"A little more than that," he responds. "Mostly because I feel self-conscious about them."

"Oh, Castor." I grip my fingers around his, noticing him instantly relax as I do, as if my touch is actually helping him. "I know it doesn't mean anything, but I like your horns." A blush rises to my cheeks as I say it.

He raises an eyebrow.

"Not like that, it's just, I don't know, like your

eyes. You have nice eyes, and you have nice horns."
My cheeks heat up even more. "That sounds really wrong."

He chuckles despite my flustering. "You think I have nice eyes?"

"Erm, arms. I meant arms. That's not actually much better, is it?"

"I suppose it depends what you're trying to do," he muses.

"Not make a fool out of myself?"

He lets out a deep laugh that almost makes it seem like he's properly relaxed, though somehow I doubt that's true. "I don't think I've ever seen you make a fool out of yourself, Sage."

"Now I know you're lying. You were around during Freshers when I decided to try and do a shot mid-cartwheel."

A bemused smile spreads over his face. "I still have to wonder why you didn't try out for the Sapphire Sparks."

"Do you remember how the cartwheel ended? If I wasn't a witch, I'd have had to go to the hospital, there's no way I'd survive even a week of being a cheerleader."

"Hmm, maybe not. You'd look cute in the uniform though."

I tuck a strand of hair behind my ear and try not

to dwell on the fact he called me cute, even if it was in the context of a hypothetical cheer squad uniform. Though he's probably not wrong.

"I'll dress up as a cheerleader next time we have a fancy dress pub crawl," I promise without thinking.

"Now that might be enough to make me agree to a night out," he jokes.

My breathing hitches. Not at the idea that he'll come out drinking with us, but more that he's saying it because of me.

A surge of people spills from the front of the academy building and Castor lets out a resigned sigh. "I guess that's my cue to get going, I have an accounting lecture to get to. I'd rather watch paint dry for an hour, but I'm not very good at it, so I need to attend all the lectures I can."

I nod. "I need to get to Spanish. Thanks for stopping to talk to me. I feel better."

"You're welcome." There's a thoughtful expression on his face, but it disappears within seconds to be replaced by a smile. "I'll probably see you back at the flat later?"

"Probably," I respond. "See you." I wave and head towards the main building. I turn around when I'm halfway there and find that Castor has done the same on his way to the business block.

He waves, causing my heart to skip a beat.

He's certainly managed to take my mind off everything with Mum, and I don't think I'll ever be able to tell him how grateful for that I am.

THREE

CASTOR

I KNOCK on Rhea's bedroom door, hoping the gorgon is around and hasn't got a late lecture or some kind of society meeting. I've been unable to stop thinking about Sage's face when I found her on the bench earlier, and that means I need to do something about it.

And her best friend is the answer. Or at least, part of it.

There's a thud from inside, followed by a hiss. "Oh shhh," Rhea scolds her snakes loudly enough that I can hear it even from here.

As self-conscious as I feel about my horns, at

least I don't have live reptiles attached to my head. Rhea's lucky she only got two, from what I've heard, gorgons can have anything from no snakes, to hundreds. I can't imagine what it must feel like to never get any peace from them.

"Sorry, I was looking for my glasses," Rhea says as she opens the door. "Don't want anyone turning into ston...oh, Castor." She frowns.

"Do you have a minute?" I ask, starting to second-guess my decision.

"Err, sure." She pulls open the door and gestures for me to step inside.

I didn't necessarily mean for her to invite me into her room, but what else is she supposed to do considering I'm standing here wanting to talk to her. She shuts the door behind me and gestures to her desk chair while she goes to sit on her bed.

I frown and take a seat, realising that this is vastly uncomfortable for both of us. "It's about Sage," I blurt out, hoping to make this a little less awkward for us both. Sage is a safe subject for us.

She raises an eyebrow and crosses her arms across her chest. "What about her?"

I clear my throat. "Has she mentioned her birthday to you?"

"Just that she's got plans with her mum. Why?" A curious expression crosses her face.

"When I ran into her earlier, she was upset that her plans fell through," I say quickly. "And she said she didn't want to call her dad and make him feel second best. So I guess I was thinking that maybe she'd like it if we threw her a birthday party. She said she might end up going on a night out with you anyway, so I guess something like that? With balloons and cake." I'm rambling, but I can't help it.

"You want to organise a birthday party for Sage?" she asks slowly.

"Yes."

"Right."

"You don't think it's a good idea?" I should have thought it through more.

"I didn't say that," Rhea responds. "I guess I'm just wondering why you'd want to do something like that."

Ah. That's the question I've been hoping to avoid, and yet I knew it was going to be the one that Rhea asked.

I clear my throat. "She's our friend, I don't want her to be unhappy."

"Mmhmm." Something on her face says she doesn't believe me.

She isn't the only one either, though I suppose I'm well aware that it's a blatant lie on my part. How can it not be when I can almost still feel my skin tingling where she touched me? I can see how people got accused of being witches because she's certainly cast some kind of spell over me. One that I'm fully accepting of.

"Okay, let's do it," she responds. "But only if she says yes to going out on Friday. If she says she wants to stay in and stuff her face with cheap wine and chocolate, then we let her."

"She said pizza and ice cream," I murmur, thinking that I should make sure to get some of both in so she can have it if she changes her mind.

"All right, so I guess I'm dealing with the invitations," Rhea says. "Anything in particular that you want to deal with?"

"The cake."

"What were you thinking?"

I shrug. "I was going to make cupcakes. Or maybe butterfly buns."

Rhea stares at me, and for a moment I wonder if she's managed to turn herself into stone, even if I think that's probably impossible. "Butterfly buns?"

"Yes, you know, the cupcakes with the tops cut in two and put on top of the buttercream so it looks like a butterfly," I say.

"I know what a butterfly bun is," Rhea responds. "I'm just trying to imagine you making them."

I shrug. "I have an eight-year-old sister, they're her favourite."

"And you bake with her?"

I nod. "Why wouldn't I?"

"No reason, I think it's really sweet that you want to make them for Sage." The way she says it makes it obvious that she thinks this is about more than me just being a good friend. And I suppose to some extent, she isn't wrong, but I would never want more than Sage is comfortable with.

I push the thoughts to the side, only for them to be replaced by the echo of her words about my horns. And my eyes. Those aren't the kinds of things you say about a friend, are they?

I don't have time to work out what all of that means *and* plan a party.

"All right, I'll start a group chat for the two of us to plan in," Rhea says. "And I'll message Sage now and ask her if she's up for going out on Friday night." She picks up her phone and types it out.

"Thanks, Rhea."

One of her snakes slithers down onto her shoulder and hisses at me.

"You are *not* hungry," she mutters to it. "Sorry about him."

"He's a he?"

She shrugs. "No idea. I don't know how to

gender real snakes, never mind snakes that live on my head. But he feels like a he, I can't explain it though."

"Magic likes to be inexplicable."

"That it does." Amusement comes through her voice.

"All right, I need to go change my shopping so I can add cake ingredients. Should I get something to drink too?"

Rhea shrugs. "Only for you, everyone knows these things are BYOB."

"BYOB?"

"Bring your own bottle," she responds. "So clearly you need to learn the rules."

I shrug. "I don't go to many parties." I get to my feet. "Thanks, Rhea, I really appreciate it."

"I haven't done anything yet," she warns me. "But you're welcome." She waves me off and turns her attention back to her snakes.

I shut her bedroom door behind me and let out a deep breath. At least that's the current hard bit out of the way. If Sage's best friend thinks that this is a good idea, then there's a chance that it actually is.

And maybe once I get it all figured out, I'll be able to put a name to the feelings growing inside me whenever I think about the pretty witch who lives in my flat and will hopefully love her birthday party.

FOUR

SAGE

WHY DID I agree to a night out? I should have l known that I was going to feel awful about the whole situation and not really be up for it. But now I've said I'm going to go, I don't want to back out and have my friends think that I don't want to hang out with them.

I sigh and step out of my room, hesitating before going to the kitchen to grab a getting-ready drink. Maybe I should go talk to Castor instead. He knew just what to say the other day when I found out that Mum had bailed on me, and I could do with some of that magic now.

Rhea's door opens and my friend's gaze falls on me. "Come on or we're going to be late."

I cock my head to the side. "Can you be late to pre-drinks?"

"You can."

I shrug, a little uncertain about what's going on with her, but if she says there's something to be late for, then I believe her.

"I just need to get something to drink," I say, heading to the kitchen.

"No!"

I stop in my tracks and turn to give her a weird look. "What's going on?"

"Would you believe me if I said nothing?" She gives me a sheepish look that suggests I've caught her in *something*, but I'm not sure what.

"Not even slightly, you're acting more freaked out than the time I walked in on you when you didn't have your glasses on," I mutter, heading towards her anyway.

"That was stressful, I could have turned you into stone."

"Only temporarily, it doesn't sound that bad." And it would have been an accident. Anyone who can't understand that is being unreasonable.

"You would say that, you've not been encased in it."

"Have you?" I ask. "I didn't think gorgon magic worked on gorgons."

"It doesn't. So no, I guess I haven't been turned into stone. But I've heard reports, and they're never good. People hate it."

"Probably because people aren't able to work on anything while they're stuck in stone. They probably get bored."

She shakes her head. "I doubt that's the reason."

"You're being fairly successful at distracting me, but I can't say I'm convinced there isn't anything going on."

Rhea sighs. "Can you just accept that something is happening, you're going to like it, and leave it at that?"

I narrow my eyes at her. "Now I'm intrigued."

"You're not supposed to be, you're not supposed to know there's anything to know." Even Rhea looks confused by what she's saying.

"Does that even make sense?"

She shrugs.

"Fine. What do I wear for this thing that I'm not supposed to know?" I ask. If I'm lucky, her answer might give me some clues about what's happening. If not, then at least I'll know what to wear.

"Something cute. Or sexy. Both. Cute and sexy."

She grabs my hand and pulls me to my bedroom without any more of an explanation.

"Okay?" I have to admit to being even more confused about what's happening now.

She sighs. "Just trust me?"

"I do."

She heads over to my wardrobe and sorts through the clothes there. "Where's that dress you bought a few months ago?"

"You're going to have to be more specific than that."

"You thought it made you look hot." She shakes her head at several of the options.

"Still more specific." I watch her with bemusement.

"Ah, here it is." She pulls out a little black dress. "*Sage*, the tag's still on."

I shrug. "I haven't had a chance to wear it yet."

"Then tonight is the perfect opportunity. Time to put it on." She shoves it at me. "Do you need to shower still?"

I nod.

"Great. Then you do that, I'm going to go get you a drink, and we'll do our hair when you're done."

Hisssssss.

"Oh shh, I'm not going to do anything to you,"

Rhea chides her snake.

I laugh lightly. "Maybe he's worried I'll set my curling iron on him."

"He shouldn't be. That thing is going nowhere near my hair, especially not my snakes. I don't want to be dealing with shedding reptiles for the next few days. Now shower, dressed," she demands. "I promise all will be revealed soon and you're going to like it."

"I'll hold you to that," I say.

"Yep, you can." She heads out of my room.

I stare at the dress she's suggested I wear and let out a sigh. There's a reason it still has the tags on, and I'm not sure today is the time to change that. But Rhea seems flustered by whatever is going on tonight, and I did promise that I'd trust her, so that's exactly what I should do. I'm going to shower and put on the dress that does make me look good, even if I feel a little self-conscious in it.

I pick up my phone and check the lock screen for what feels like the hundredth time. No new messages, meaning that Mum hasn't just disappeared off to Paris with her new boyfriend, but she's completely forgotten about my birthday. Somehow, that's worse than if she spent the day complaining about how she should get presents because she's the one who gave birth to me.

I push those thoughts from my mind. She might have forgotten, but plenty of people haven't. Dad messaged me at six in the morning, and my friends have all wished me happy birthday in one way or another. It's not even about the fact she's missed my birthday. I know that birthdays aren't that big of a deal at nineteen, it's more that she's completely forgotten what she promised, and not even given me any thought. I drop my phone onto the bed with a frustrated sigh and try not to let it get to me more than it already has.

Instead, I'm going to focus on whatever it is Rhea is planning. I don't even know how she knew to plan anything, the only person I told about Mum bailing was Castor, and it's not like he'll have told her. I don't think I've ever seen the two of them have a conversation without the rest of us around.

I glance at the dress she picked out. I suppose it wouldn't hurt to wear a dress like that if he could see me. It definitely *seems* like Rhea's right and he's more interested in me.

Before I have a chance to second-guess myself, I jump into the shower and start getting ready for a night of fun with my friends. Some outrageous drinking games and the chance to dance the night away sound like just the thing to chase away the echo of disappointment lingering within me.

FIVE

CASTOR

I CHECK the buns to make sure they're cool enough to ice and start taking off the tops. I should be done by now, especially with the party starting in half an hour, but this is where I'm up to, so I'm just going to have to go with it. Anything to make sure that Sage's party goes off without a hitch, though I am starting to worry about whether this was a good idea. What if she hates it?

The kitchen door swings open and I look up in a panic, only a little relieved to find Rhea stepping inside. She's not dressed properly yet, which is reassuring.

"You're still baking?" she asks.

"My first batch of buns went wrong, so I remade them," I respond. "I'm ready other than that though." I gesture to my shirt, though it's currently covered with an apron.

She nods approvingly. "Well, Sage might have already figured out I'm up to something, though I can't imagine she's going to arrive at the conclusion that you're organising a party for her. I have to make her a drink now or she's going to end up coming in here early."

I shrug. "It was bound to happen."

"Oh, and I brought these." She sets a packet of brightly coloured cardboard on the table and tears it open. A few seconds later, she's folding one of them into a party hat and holding it out to me.

"I'm not sure that's my style," I say, eyeing it warily.

"It will be when you see the dress Sage is going to wear," Rhea mutters under her breath.

I consider asking her why she'd think that, but I know better than to poke at that particular train of thought.

"It's just a party hat," Rhea says.

"All right, but if no one else puts one on, I'm taking it off."

"That's a fair deal."

I take it from her and pull the elastic under my chin, settling it on my head between my horns. "How do I look?"

"Honestly?"

"Why else would I ask?" And I'm already aware of the answer. I can't imagine a party hat is going to look good between my horns.

One of her snakes slithers onto her shoulder and gives a soft hiss. She shrugs. "Some people don't want to hear the answer."

"Well, I do."

"Okay, then you look a little ridiculous, but I think Sage will love it," she says honestly.

A smile spreads over my face before I can stop it, receiving a knowing look from Rhea.

"Mmhmm, thought as much," she says as she goes over to the fridge and pulls out some cranberry juice, no doubt to make the drink she promised to take to Sage.

"I didn't say anything," I mumble.

"Look, I know we don't know each other that well, but a little piece of advice? If you like Sage, tell her."

"I don't want to make her uncomfortable." It's the first time I've admitted it out loud. But Rhea has been helping me with this for days, and she wouldn't be suggesting something she didn't think Sage would be open to, would she?

"Trust me, I don't want to live in a flat with two people awkwardly making small talk either. So *tell her.*" The way she stresses the last part makes me think she's trying to say more than the words actually mean.

A soft hiss comes from her snake.

Rhea sighs. "If you don't stop that, I'll put you in a party hat too."

The snake looks alarmed, which is impressive considering that it's a snake, and slithers back up into her hair.

"I think he's got the right idea," I mutter.

Rhea laughs. "I'm sure he does." She finishes off the drink. "Right, I'm going to take this to Sage and see how she's getting on. How long do you need?"

"Maybe another ten or twenty minutes?"

"Good, 'cause that's all you've really got. Everyone should start arriving soon."

I nod even as she turns and disappears out of the kitchen door.

I sigh and look over the slight mess I seem to have made with the cakes. It'll be fine. It's not like anyone will care, and I can just get one of the witches to clean it up with a flick of their wand when they arrive. It must be nice to have magic that's actually useful.

I reach up and touch one of my horns, feeling the hard ridges as I do. It's strange, but I'm convinced they aren't bothering me as much as they were before my talk with Sage on the bench. Maybe because someone I think of as a friend thinks they're nice.

Though that's if I don't lie to myself about my feelings. Considering I'm standing in the middle of an icing sugar explosion and I'm wearing a party hat, I can't even pretend that there's no truth in what Rhea is saying.

I would love to be more than just Sage's friend, I just don't know how to make it happen. I suppose that this is a good start. At least her reaction will tell me how she's feeling about me. Maybe.

I try to keep my thoughts on making the cakes, carefully constructing them to look like butterflies and putting them on the stand. I haven't done this for anyone except my sister, but the more cakes I put on the cardboard stand, the more certain I get that this is going to make her night. She'd been so heartbroken when I saw her on the bench, and I know I can't make her mum come to take her out for dinner, but at least I think I can bring a smile to her face.

The doorbell goes just as I'm putting the final cake on the stand and I let out a sigh of relief. I dump the buttercream bowl in the sink, intent on dealing with it later, and pull off my apron. The material tugs as it gets stuck on my horns and I let out an annoyed grunt as I untangle the situation. I should get an apron that ties around the back of my neck so this doesn't happen again.

I finally manage to get it off as the kitchen door opens and people start streaming in. I don't know many of them very well, but I recognise some from lectures and from other parties we've had here. Someone finds the bag of party hats that Reha left on the table and starts handing them out, which at least makes me feel a little less self-conscious than I did before.

I just hope Sage loves this as much as I think she's going to.

SIX

SAGE

I SMOOTH down my dress and try to ignore how weirdly nervous I am. My mind goes to the barely-touched vodka cranberry sitting on my desk. I'm not sure why I didn't drink more of it while getting ready, especially as it would probably have helped with the confidence in my current outfit.

"Are you going to tell me what I'm walking into?" I ask Rhea.

She snorts. "Nope."

"That's mean."

"You're going to like it. And by the way, none of

this was my idea." There's a smug expression on her face that is confusing given her statement.

"Are you telling me that because you don't want me to blame you if it goes badly?" I joke.

"I'm telling you that so you give credit to the right person," she responds cryptically.

"I have so many questions."

"Maybe that's the point." One of her snakes slithers onto her shoulder and lets out a gentle hiss. "I'll still put a party hat on you," she chides it.

I guess that confirms one of my theories about what I'm going to find when I enter the kitchen.

I push open the door and step inside.

"Surprise!" The cheer is louder than I expect it to be, and I stand there in stunned silence as I take in the scene in front of me. A banner with *Happy Birthday Sage* hangs across the large window, and the kitchen table is covered in bottles and brightly coloured cups.

All of my flatmates are here, as well as several people from WitchSoc, and others that I don't think I even know. I'm guessing the guests brought guests, that's always how these things go.

"Hey," I say, waving awkwardly. I've always wondered how it feels to be the person being surprised at a party like this. I suppose I'm getting a first-hand experience of it now.

Rhea chuckles and throws an arm around my shoulder. "Surprised?"

"You managed to keep this quiet almost until the last moment."

"That's because I'm not the mastermind." She nods over to where a large cake stand filled with what look like butterfly buns sits on the kitchen counter.

But it's not the cake that catches my attention, but the minotaur standing next to them with a full glass in his hand and a nervous expression on his face.

"Castor did this?" My voice cracks with emotion as I ask.

"He did."

"Why?"

"Why do you think?" There's amusement in her voice.

"He knew I was upset about Mum, I guess."

Rhea snorts. "The two of you deserve each other."

"Hey, what's that supposed to mean?" I turn to my best friend and cross my arms.

"It means that you're both ignoring the fact that you're really obviously into each other. Come on, Sage. He's organised you a birthday party because you were sad." She gives me a look that makes me certain she wants me to put the pieces together. "How about I distract everyone with a drinking game, and you go have a moment with your minotaur."

"He's not mine."

"Come back to me again on that tomorrow," she teases.

My heart constricts at the thought. I do *like* the idea of that statement changing.

I nod and start making my way over to where Castor is standing, barely paying any attention to the people gathered here, which I know is bad when they're here to see me, but they're not what's most important right now. I'll say hi to them once I've talked with Castor.

I come to a stop in front of him and realise my heart is pounding harder than I think it ever has before. "Hey."

He clears his throat. "Hi."

"Thank you."

He blinks.

"For the party. Rhea said you put this together."

"Oh, you're welcome," he murmurs.

"It's really thoughtful." I reach out to touch his arm but pause before I get there. It was nice to take his hand the other day, but I don't know if I'm brave enough to initiate physical contact now.

"I didn't do much. I just asked for Rhea's help," he says.

"And wore a party hat."

He touches it. "How bad does it look?"

"It's cute," I assure him. "But it's wonky. Can I?"

He nods.

I bite my lip and reach up to straighten it, my hand accidentally brushing against his horn as I do. He stiffens and I instantly worry that I've done the wrong thing.

"I'm sorry." I pull back.

"It's okay, it was nice. I think."

"Do people touch your horns a lot?" I ask without thinking, then close my eyes. "That sounded really dirty."

He chuckles. "It did."

"I didn't mean it to, I was asking about the horns on your head."

"As opposed to the horns I have elsewhere?" he teases, a glint of amusement in his voice.

My cheeks flush. "I don't even know how to answer that. Do you even have horns elsewhere?"

"Wouldn't you like to know?"

"Yes."

Oops. I didn't mean for that to slip out. The

word hangs between us, with neither of us quite knowing what to do with it.

Castor rubs the back of his neck, a slightly nervous expression crossing his face, and I have to wonder what's going through his head. Maybe Rhea's wrong and he doesn't like me as anything more than a friend and he's embarrassed about being caught up in a flirty moment and doesn't want to give me the wrong impression.

Or maybe he just doesn't know how to broach the subject.

"The cakes look good," I say when it's clear that neither of us are going to say anything else. "I haven't had butterfly buns in ages." I pick one up and swipe my finger through the buttercream to eat it.

Castor's gaze fixates on me and it's only then that I realise what I've done. Somehow, I'm making a complete mess out of the entire interaction when I'm supposed to be thanking him for the party.

"It's really good," I say sheepishly.

"My sister loves it when I make them for her," he says.

"You made these?" My eyes widen. Okay, there's no way Rhea's wrong about the situation.

"I did."

"So you *did* do more than wear a party hat and ask Rhea for help!"

He lets out a nervous laugh. "Yeah, I guess I did."

Feeling a little bolder, I go up on my toes and press a kiss to his cheek. "Thank you."

He raises his hand to his cheek, a slightly dazed expression on his face. "You're welcome," he grumbles.

Not knowing what else to do, I eat some more of my bun. It's delicious, I hope I can convince him to make these again. Or that I get to find out what else he's good at baking.

I'm almost ready to ask when he clears his throat. "I need to..." he waves towards the door vaguely.

Before I can fully process what's happening, he's weaving through people and out of the kitchen in a way that I'm reasonably sure is just to get away from me. I try not to let the hurt set in.

Clearly, this is something we need to talk about.

Without thinking twice about it, I follow him, making my way through the assembled people and out into the hallway. I hurry down to Castor's bedroom and knock on the door.

"Castor? Please let me in. Can we talk?" My

palms are sweating and I can't help but worry about what's going to happen when he opens the door.

Or what will happen if he doesn't.

But I know that we need to talk now. How can we not when he's done all of this just to make me feel better?

SEVEN

Castor

What was I thinking?

This whole party was a bad idea. Sage probably thinks it's awful.

Though that's not what her face said when she walked in, or when she came straight over to me. My heart does a traitorous flutter and my hand goes to my cheek where she kissed me.

Somehow, this has gotten a little bit more complicated.

A knock sounds on my bedroom door and I freeze.

"Castor? Please let me in. Can we talk?" Sage calls.

What do I do? I *want* to talk to her, but I'm worried about what she's going to say. I don't know if I can face the rejection I have no doubt is about to come.

"Castor?" The heartbroken note in her voice is enough to sway me and I head over to the door. I pause for a moment and count to three, trying to keep myself calm.

I pull open the door, my heart constricting more at the sight of the beautiful witch standing on the other side.

"Can I come in?" she asks.

I nod and step back.

She brushes against me, leaving the scent of her perfume lingering in the air. I swallow hard. This is going to be difficult if she's going to be so distracting.

I close the door, suddenly aware that she's in my bedroom. It's not the first time I've thought of this happening, but this isn't exactly how I imagined it.

She takes a deep breath. "What happened?" she asks softly, still standing in the middle of my room and looking like she might run away.

"I panicked," I admit.

"Okay." She takes a deep breath. "I'm sorry if I made you uncomfortable."

"You didn't. I was uncomfortable because of my own thoughts."

She raises an eyebrow. "What kind of thoughts?"

"I'd rather not say."

Sage steps closer. "I could guess?"

"I don't think you could."

A knowing smile spreads over her face, and it's only once she's looking up at me that I realise how close she now is. "I like you," she says.

I hear the words, but they don't compute.

"It's hard to admit this stuff out loud when I don't know how you're going to respond. But here it goes. I have a huge crush on you, and I'd like to do something about it," she says. "If you want that too."

"You're just saying this because you've been drinking," I mumble.

"I think I managed two sips of the vodka cranberry Rhea made me earlier, and you saw that I didn't drink anything while I was in the kitchen. So I'm definitely sober enough to know how I'm feeling. This isn't something new because I've been drinking, or because you threw me a party, though I guess that is why I'm telling you."

"You like the party?"

"I *love* the party, Castor. It was such a sweet gesture."

"I wanted to cheer you up."

"I know. And that means a lot to me. I guess I'm just wondering..." She trails off and glances away.

"What are you wondering?" he asks.

"What it means to you," she says firmly. "Did you do this because we're friends and I was sad? Or did you do it for another reason?"

I consider the question, mostly because I want to work out what the right answer is. "I did it because I thought you'd like it."

"Right."

"And I guess because I like you."

Her whole face lights up. "You do?"

"Yes. But I didn't do it because I expected anything. I guess that's why I ran away, I didn't want you to think that I expected anything in return."

"But if I was to do something like kiss you, you wouldn't be opposed to it?"

I chuckle deeply, feeling a lot more at ease now things are starting to be out in the open. "I wouldn't be opposed to it."

She goes up on her toes and kisses my left cheek. "What about now?"

"I like it."

"Mmhmm." She moves to the other side and I know she's going to kiss my right cheek.

Feeling bold, I turn and capture her lips with mine instead. She responds instantly, wrapping her arms around my neck and pressing herself against me.

I circle my arms around her waist and lose myself in the way it feels to be finally kissing her. The way she's responding makes it clear that everything she's said is true, and I feel as if I can finally let go of the worry that's been holding me back.

Sage pulls back but doesn't leave my arms. "And now?" she whispers, looking up at me with large hopeful eyes.

I clear my throat. "Now I think that one kiss might not be enough."

"Oh good." She doesn't waste a moment and kisses me again.

All of my thoughts are chased away, and I can't help but feel as if a weight has been lifted from my shoulders.

"We should get back to the party," I murmur once we've broken apart again.

"I thought you didn't like parties."

"I might change my mind," I admit. "But this one is different anyway, everyone came for you."

She sighs and finally leaves my arms.

They feel empty without her.

"I guess you're right." She reaches out and takes my hand in hers as she heads towards my bedroom door. "So, are you going to ask me on a date, or are we just going to wait for the next party to make out in your room again?"

I snort. "Then I'd *really* like parties."

She smiles knowingly at me, but stops before we enter the kitchen.

"What are you doing tomorrow?" I ask.

"Well, it's Saturday."

"Ah, so you'll put on a movie marathon and eat pizza from the place down the road," I say without thinking.

"Yep. Want to join me?" She bites her bottom lip.

"Does that count as a date?"

"If we say it does."

"Then it's a date," I respond, checking through the glass to make sure no one's watching before pulling her back towards me and kissing her again. It's not that I need to keep what we're doing a secret, but I want to make sure she has the chance to tell people in her own time.

She kisses me back, and I can tell that it's not going to be anywhere near the last time we do this.

We break apart and she looks up at me as if there aren't over a dozen people in the next room.

"We should go back inside."

"Yep."

She nods and takes a deep breath, stepping inside and heading over to a group of her friends.

I follow, uncertain about what I'm going to do now. I suppose I should get a drink. It *is* a party after all.

I head over to the fridge and grab myself a beer, looking over to where Sage is chatting with some of the others. She looks up and smiles at me, making my heart constrict in the best way.

It turns out that throwing a party is precisely what I needed to do in order to find out if there's anything between us.

"So, I'm guessing that went well?" Rhea's question breaks through my thoughts.

"Hmm?" I turn to the gorgon, unsurprised to find her leaning against the kitchen side with a bemused and satisfied expression on her face.

"You and Sage disappeared about twenty minutes ago, and now you're both back and you're grinning from ear to ear. If I didn't know you both better, then I'd have thought you snuck away for a quickie."

I stare at her, not entirely sure how to respond to that.

"I'm happy for you." She pats my arm. "And just so you know, I'll be asking Sage *a lot* of questions." She winks at me and walks off before I can question her further about that. Though if I'm honest, I'm not entirely sure I want the answers.

I lean against the kitchen side and let out a contented sigh. Of all the ways I expected tonight to go, this wasn't it.

But I can't say I'm sad about that.

EIGHT

SAGE

ONE OF MY fellow witches almost trips on her way out of the door and down to the taxis that are going to take them to the nightclub.

I try to refrain from laughing, knowing that I've done the same more than once. She cackles loudly, and I'm a little relieved that she's finding it funny.

"Are you sure you're not coming?" Rhea asks.

I shake my head and glance back at the kitchen door. I know it's a real mess beyond. "I'm going to help Castor clean up."

"Mmhmm." She gives me a knowing look, as does one of her snakes.

"I am."

"We both know that you can have that done in thirty seconds."

"It'll take a bit longer than that, even with magic," I point out. "I'm not drunk enough to go party."

"That's because you've had two drinks all night. I'd say you're trying to keep a clear head for something." She wiggles her eyebrows suggestively.

"All right, just go drink and try not to turn anyone into stone. You took your gorgon potion, right?" The last thing either of us needs is for her to be calling me at three am and asking me to help her because she's turned someone into a temporary rock.

She snorts. "Do you think I'd have had three vodkas if I hadn't?"

"You've had six," I tell my friend. "Now have fun, message me."

"Pfft, you're not going to be paying any attention to your messages."

"Do it all the same, that way I know you're safe," I say firmly.

"Okay, fineeeee. I'm going to go dance, and you're going to go...hmm, there's no way to make that rhyme." She cocks her head to the side.

"I'm going to go *clean*," I stress.

"Now there's a euphemism I've never used before. Oh, but I could use it. Maybe I need someone to *snake my drain*."

I wrinkle my nose. "Rhea! Ew, why? No, never say that again."

She laughs maniacally. "I can't promise anything."

"You really should. Now go, or you'll miss the taxi," I say, pushing her towards the door.

"Stay safe, Sage."

"You too." I shut the flat door behind her and try to shake the image she put in my head loose before heading back to the kitchen. I can hear Castor moving around, and I don't want him to think that he has to clean up as well as organise everything, especially when I can do it much faster. Though thirty seconds is still a little bit of a stretch.

I push open the door and step inside.

He looks up, seemingly surprised that I'm still here.

"Let me do that," I say, pulling out my wand.

"You don't have to, it's your birthday," he responds.

"Only for another twenty minutes."

Indecision wars on his face.

"It won't take long." I hold up my wand to

remind him that I'm perfectly capable of doing it much easier.

"All right." He steps back from the mess of cups and sticky spilt alcohol all over the table.

I grimace. "It doesn't look anywhere near as fun as it was."

He chuckles. "So long as it was fun, though."

I look at him and smile. "I had the best time." I wave my wand over the table, clearing the discarded cups and bottles into the bin.

A second spell has the stickiness disappearing in front of our eyes.

"I have to admit, that's a useful trick. Our flat's probably cleaner than my mum's kitchen, and that says something," Castor jokes.

I shrug. "Being a witch has some advantages." I move around the kitchen cleaning everything away and feeling a deep sense of achievement in how quickly and effectively it's doing it. "Okay, all done, I think." I slip my wand back into my pocket.

"I guess so," he says, shifting from one foot to the other.

"Just one thing left," I say, going to my cupboard and pulling out a small bottle and two glasses. I pour some of the potion into each of them and hold one out to him. "Here."

"What is it?" he asks.

"Well, you seemed bothered earlier about the fact that I might have been drinking when we were talking. So I'm getting ahead of that. This will sober us up." I've not drunk very much to begin with, but now that things seem to be going somewhere with Castor, I don't want to mess it up.

He raises an eyebrow. "I didn't realise there was a potion that did that."

"If it's a desired effect, a witch somewhere has worked out how to make a potion for it," I respond. "And this one works like a treat. It's more expensive than hangover cures though, so I only use it when it's important."

"Will it work on me?"

"Should do. Rhea's used it before. Remember when she had that Art History exam and she was still drunk in the morning?"

He lets out a small laugh. "She was a mess."

"Mmhmm."

"All right, then cheers." He holds his glass out to me.

I tap mine against his and down the potion, trying not to think about how bitter it is. Despite the fact I haven't had very much to drink, my head still feels clearer the moment the potion hits my system.

Castor winces as his goes down. "You could have warned me about the taste," he mutters.

"It's not that bad."

"Sure," he mutters.

"I can make it better," I promise, taking the glass out of his hand and stepping closer to him.

"Oh?"

I go up on my toes and wrap my arms around his neck.

His hand rests on the small of my back and I can feel the warmth seeping into me.

My gaze flits to his lips, and he takes it as the invitation it is to lean in and kiss me. I can taste the remnants of the potion on him, but I don't care. Kissing him is intoxicating in a whole different way. There's a small part of me that can't believe that this is actually happening and that I'm finally getting what I wanted. I know it's just the beginning, but I can sense that this is something that's going to last.

I break away from him and look up, seeing the same thing written in his eyes.

"I don't want tonight to end," he murmurs.

"It doesn't have to," I respond, trailing my hand along his arm.

"You already did all the cleaning," he points out.

"I wasn't thinking about cleaning, Castor." I bite my bottom lip, trying to think of the right way to put this that doesn't sound as awfully crude as the way Rhea put it.

"Oh." Understanding dawns in his eyes. "*Oh.*"

"Only if you want to," I say quickly.

"Are you sure?"

"Why do you think I wanted to make sure we were completely sober?" I ask. "I wanted to make sure that we were sure."

"I see."

"But no pressure. If you don't want to, then we can just..." I trail off because I'm not entirely sure what we can *just* do.

He pulls me closer and gazes deep into my eyes. "I don't want tonight to end," he repeats.

"Okay." I take his hand and pull him towards the kitchen door, excitement replacing all the nerves I felt earlier.

Somehow, this has turned into one of my best birthdays ever, even if it started out as one of the worst.

EPILOGUE

SAGE

A Year Later

I FIDDLE with the hem of my cardigan nervously while we wait outside the restaurant for my mum to show up. A part of me wonders if she's going to bail on me again like she did last year. It could become a birthday tradition. Or maybe it already is one. She's been fairly consistent my entire life, why change now?

"You're nervous," Castor says, putting his arm around me and pulling me closer.

"You know I am." But I feel better having him with me.

"You can touch my horns, if you want," he offers.

I snort. "Is that your way of distracting me?"

He shrugs. "You seem to like it."

I reach up and touch the hard curve of his horn where it juts out from his skull, following the curve upwards. There's something soothing about running my fingers over the ridges, though I don't know why. I suppose it doesn't matter.

I let out a contented sigh. "Thank you."

He chuckles. "You're welcome to touch my horns any time."

I bite my bottom lip. "You know I'm going to take you up on that."

"I'm counting on it, it is your birthday after all."

"Which means it's also our anniversary," I respond.

"It is." He pulls me closer and captures my lips with his, kissing me gently. "I love you, Sage."

"I love you too," I respond instantly, feeling the same glow of warmth within me as every time he's said it to me. It's hard to believe that barely a year ago we were still dancing around one another and neither of us had admitted how we were feeling about one another out loud.

I sigh and lean my head against his chest.

"Has she messaged?" he asks.

I pull out my phone to check, but shake my head. "Not yet. But that's not a huge surprise. We'll give it another ten minutes, and if she doesn't show up we'll go home and I'll eat ten of the butterfly buns you made me."

He snorts. "Or we could just go for dinner ourselves."

"I suppose I could agree to that."

"But I think you're going to be okay." He gestures in the other direction.

I unpeel myself from his arms and turn in time to see my mum getting out of a taxi, thankfully alone. I'm not sure what I'd have done if she'd brought her *new* new boyfriend with her. I know it's a good thing that she's trying to move on after the divorce, I just wish I didn't have to deal with her poor taste in men.

"Sagey, honey," she says, hurrying over and pulling me into a hug. "I can't believe my baby is twenty."

"Me neither, Mum." I already feel more tense with her presence, which I hate, but have no idea how to change.

She kisses my cheeks and pulls back. "And you must be Castor, we finally get a chance to meet," she says.

I bite my tongue and refrain from pointing out

that she's had several chances to meet him, she's just been constantly blowing me off every time we have plans. Dad met him a couple of months after we started dating.

"It's nice to meet you, Ms Anders," he says.

"Oh don't call me that, it makes me sound old, you must call me Terri." She looks at him in a way I really don't like. "You've done well for yourself, Sagey."

I flash Castor an apologetic smile. "Shall we go inside?" I don't want to encourage Mum by responding to her comment.

"I'm serious. I dated a minotaur once. Well, dated is a strong word, but wow was it the time of my life." She smiles in a way that makes me feel deeply uncomfortable.

"Mum! Please stop?"

"What? I'm just approving of your boyfriend. You know you don't have to settle down yet, you can do some experimenting. If you haven't tried a vampire yet..."

"Mum," I say sharply.

"Right, sorry, we're here for dinner." She almost skips into the restaurant.

I take a deep breath. "I'm sorry," I murmur to Castor.

He takes my hand in his and gives it a reassuring squeeze. "That's okay, I was expecting it."

"Even so..."

"You're worth it, Sage," he promises. "Now let's go have dinner with your mum, and when we get back to the flat, we can celebrate just the two of us."

I smile, reassured by his steady presence. With him by my side, I know that my birthday is going to be good no matter what happens when we go inside.

THANK you for reading *Party Hats For Sweet Minotaurs*, I hope you enjoyed it! If you want to read more from the Obscure Academy series, why not start with *Shifting Forms For Clumsy Felines*, which follows Krissi, a cheerleading leopard shifter who is determined to ignore her attraction to her flatmate, Jeremy: https://books2read.com/shiftingformsforclumsyfelines

AUTHOR NOTE

Thank you for reading *Party Hats For Sweet Minotaurs*, I hope you enjoyed it!

I never planned this story, it was actually a result of a game one of my author friends played during a party in The Paranormal Council group on Facebook. We were joking and saying that minotaurs in party hats would be a fun idea and sounded like something I'd write. Sometimes, the creative brain is just going to do what the creative brain is going to do, and before I knew it, there was a fun story for Sage and Castor!

If you're wondering about Rhea and her snakes, she will have a story in the Obscure Academy series, but it is yet to be announced! However, if you're interested in learning more about gorgons, you can in *Blind Dates For Lonely Gorgons*!

If you want to keep up to date with new releases and other news, you can join my Facebook Reader Group or mailing list.

Stay safe & happy reading!

- Laura

Signed Paperback & Merchandise:

You can find signed paperbacks, hardcovers, and merchandise based on my series (including stickers, magnets, face masks, and more!) via my website: https://www.authorlauragreenwood.co.uk/p/shop.html

Series List:

* denotes a completed series

The Obscure World

A paranormal & urban fantasy world where supernaturals live out in the open alongside humans. Each series can be read on its own, but there are cameos from past characters and mentions of previous events.

Cauldron Coffee Shop - Broomstick Bakery - Obscure Academy - The Shifter Season - Grimalkin Academy* - City Of Blood* - Grimalkin Vampires* - Supernatural Retrieval Agency* - Sabre Woods Academy* - Scythe Grove Academy*

* * *

The Forgotten Gods World

A fantasy romance world based on Egyptian mythology. Each series can be read on its own, but there are cameos from past characters and mentions of previous events.

Forgotten Gods

* * *

The Egyptian Empire

A modern fantasy world set in an alternative timeline where the Egyptian Empire never fell.

The Apprentice Of Anubis

* * *

The Paranormal Council Universe

A paranormal romance & urban fantasy world where paranormals are hidden away from the human world, and are in search of their fated mates. Each series can be read on its own, but there are cameos from past characters and mentions of previous events.

The Paranormal Council Series* - Paranormal Criminal Investigations* - The Necromancer Council*

Other Series

Amethyst's Wand Shop Mysteries (with Arizona Tape) - Purple Oasis (with Arizona Tape) - Grimm Academy - Beyond The Curse* - The Vampire Detective* (with Arizona Tape) - The Dragon Duels* - Speed Dating With The Denizens Of The Underworld (shared world) - Seven Wardens* (with Skye MacKinnon) - Firehouse Witches* (with Lacey Carter Andersen & L.A. Boruff)

ABOUT LAURA GREENWOOD

Laura is a USA Today Bestselling Author of paranormal, fantasy, urban fantasy, and contemporary romance. When she's not writing, she drinks a lot of tea, tries to resist French macarons, and works towards a diploma in Egyptology. She lives in the UK, where most of her books are set. Laura specialises in quick reads, whether you're looking for a swoonworthy romance for the bath, or an action-packed adventure for your latest journey, you'll find the perfect match amongst her books!

Follow the Author

- Website: www.authorlauragreenwood. co.uk
- Mailing List: www. authorlauragreenwood.co.uk/p/mailing- list-sign-up.html
- Facebook Group: http://facebook.com/ groups/theparanormalcouncil

- Facebook Page: http://facebook.com/authorlauragreenwood
- Bookbub: www.bookbub.com/authors/laura-greenwood